A MAGIC CIRCLE BOOK

small garden

BIG SURPRISE

story and pictures by **JAN ADKINS**

THEODORE CLYMER
SENIOR AUTHOR, READING 360

XEROX

GINN AND COMPANY
A XEROX EDUCATION COMPANY

garden

tomatoes

lettuce

onions

cucumbers

corn

carrots

carrot?

carrot!

CARROT